to:

from:

for Ed

Published by Schwartz & Wade Books, an imprint of Random House
Children's Books, a division of Random House, Inc., New York
Copyright © 2008 by Rebecca Doughty
All rights reserved.
Schwartz & Wade Books and colophon are trademarks of Random House, Inc.
Visit us on the Web! www.randomhouse.com/kids
Educators and librarians, for a variety of teaching tools, visit us at
www.randomhouse.com/teachers

Library of Congress Cataloging-in-Publication Data
Doughty, Rebecca.
Some helpful tips for a better world and a happier life / Rebecca Doughty. – 1st ed.
p. cm.
Summary: Offers suggestions on how to improve life, from trying new things
and splashing in puddles to making funny faces in the mirror.
ISBN 978-0-375-84272-6 (trade) – ISBN 978-0-375-94555-7 (lib. bdg.)
[1. Conduct of life–Fiction.] I. Title.

PZ7.D7448So 2008
[E]–dc22

2007019362

The illustrations in this book are rendered in ink and Flashe paint.

PRINTED IN CHINA
10 9 8 7 6 5 4 3 2 1
First Edition

Some Helpful TiPs for a
BETTER
WORLD
and a Happier Life

written and
illustrated by
Rebecca Doughty

schwartz & wade books · new york

Begin each day

by making

funny faces

in the mirror.

oo la la !

Experiment
with your
hairdo.

Make music

and A R T.

Make Cupcakes.

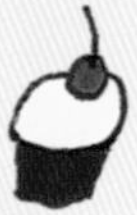

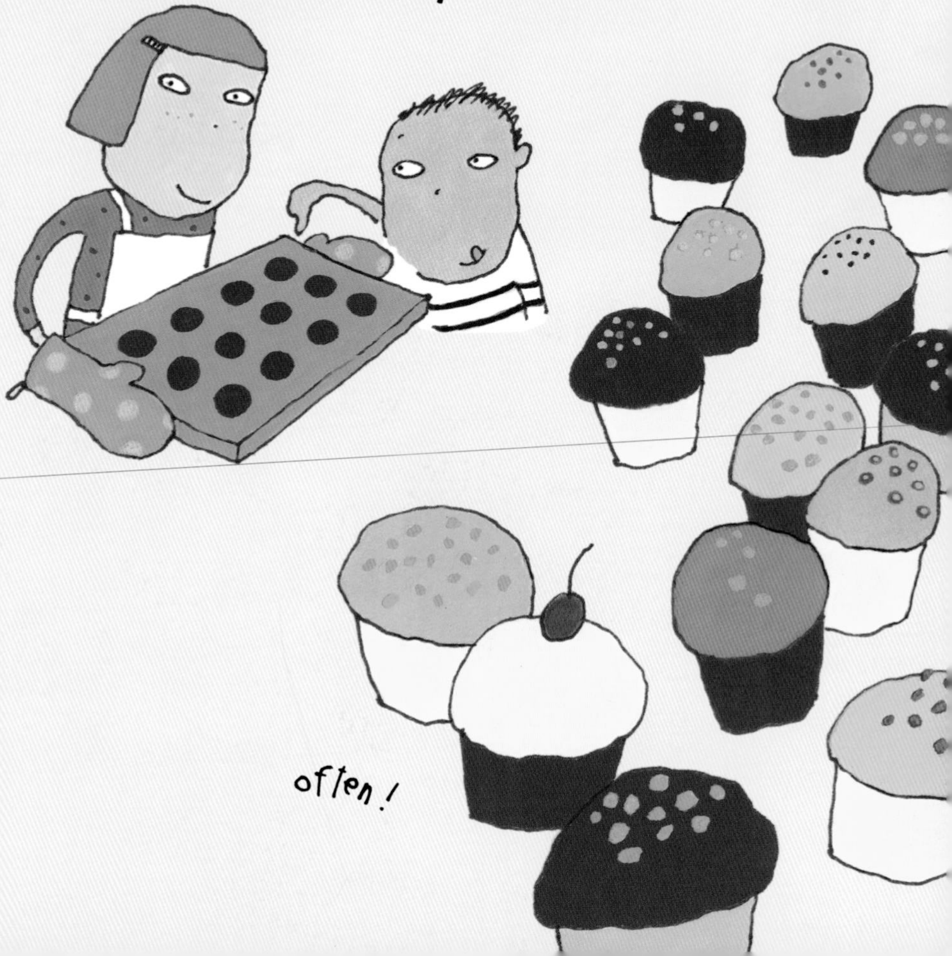

often!

Make wishes.

Invent
occasions
for
CelebRations.

Try new things.

Talk to somebody new.

Lend Mother Nature a hand.

go
go

busy
busy

argue
argue

rush
rush
hurry

blame
blame

blah
blah

STOP

and smell the flowers.

SPLASH in puddles

whenever possible.

EAT YOUR VEGETABLES!

Find someone you can always tell
your troubles to...

...and who can tell you theirs.

Read.

Dance.

Be  YOU.